Fall Into You

A SEASON FOR LOVE BOOK 1

GEORGINA KIERSTEN

THE MAGNIFICENT ENGINE

To Starr, the one who lights the way for me, and to my beloved mother who always knew I would get here.

Foreword

Fall Into You was supposed to be a simple story of Black queer love and fat acceptance. It was a story that although deeply personal to me, was simply a shot of happiness in an otherwise dark place. This book had all the things that I loved wrapped up into a tiny novella.

Looking back, when I had initially outlined this book in an hour with every intention to submit it to an Autumn themed romance anthology; it never occurred to me that 'Fall Into You' would change my life.

A year later, I am overwhelmed and deeply grateful for all the support this book has gotten. 'Fall Into You' has opened so many doors for me and touched so many other lives. In an industry where the common knowledge is that Black fat people on the cover don't sell. The hundreds of readers of 'Fall Into You' have proven them wrong.

It turns out that there *is* a need for simple cozy Black fat queer romances.

I want to thank all of my readers for taking a chance on my book and for loving Imari and Cassidy as much as I do.

Contents

Chapter One

Season of mists and mellow fruitfulness,
Close bosom-friend of the maturing sun;
Conspiring with him how to load and bless.
— To Autumn by John Keats

IMARI FELT NOTHING BUT DREAD AT THE SICKENING FAMIL-IAR RINGTONE that echoed through her tiny studio apartment. She groaned, disturbing her cat, who lay next to her. Bramble gave a very affronted yowl for messing with him.

Imari would apologize later.

She hid underneath the warm comfortable duvet, protecting herself against the cool chill of the November morning. Imari waited, biting her lip as the phone rang and rang.

After what seemed like forever, Imari closed her eyes in relief as the phone went suddenly silent. Honestly, she wanted to hide here forever.

Imari winced as very sharp claws dug through her fleece pajama pants.

The phone rang again, and with a tired sigh, Imari threw the covers off of her and, with shaking hands, grabbed her phone. Imari's stomach churned with anxiety as she looked at the display.

Mom.

Imari closed her eyes and took a deep breath. Her fingers paused between the accept or decline button. She bit her lip and tapped on the green button.

"You finally answered." Her mother said, sharply.

Imari winced. "S-sorry, I was sleeping."

"At this time of day?" Her mother said, affronted. "The sluggard does not plow in the autumn; he will seek at harvest and have nothing."

Of course, her mother would start with the Bible quotes.

"Imari Elizabeth Haines--"

"Mom?" Imari interrupted tiredly. "What did you need?"

"What I need is a daughter who will show more respect for me than telling me three weeks from Thanksgiving that they weren't coming and in an email, no less!"

Imari winced. She knew sending that email was a mistake but it was the only way Imari could tell her mother without being talked into going to yet another painful family dinner. Especially after what happened earlier this year.

"I'm sorry--"

"You should be sorry, Imari. I didn't raise you to be a lazy coward, but yet here we are."

Those words sliced her to the core, as her mother's words often did. Imari's eyes stung with unshed tears.

"IMARI ARE YOU LISTENING TO ME?!"

"Yes, ma'am."

"You already embarrassed this family enough with your theatrics. You will not embarrass me by not showing up. God knows what the neighbors will say--"

'No,' Imari thought to herself. '*I will not let you put me on display like some kind of zoo animal.*' She opened her mouth, but in the end, all she could do was sit there as her mother berated her for all her shortcomings.

Bramble butted against her hand, and Imari absent-mindedly petted her cat's black, orange, and white fur.

Imari sighed in relief when there was a knock at the door.

"Mom--" Imari interrupted. "Someone is at the door. I'll call you later."

She hung up and with a weary sigh, Imari adjusted the teal-colored bonnet on her head and stomped out of her bedroom and to the door.

Standing in the doorway, holding a white paper bag and two styrofoam cups was her best friend, Zephyr.

"You're not ready!"

"Um, yeah, I just got up."

Zephyr looked up at the ceiling and shook his head. "You forgot! I can't believe that you forgot. Today is the apple festival."

Imari gasped, "Oh my god--"

"We were supposed to be set up in fifteen minutes."

"I'm so, so sorry." Imari sighed. "I kind of had a rough morning."

Zephyr set his things down on the floor. He pushed his sunglasses on top of his head. "Imari, what's wrong?"

Imari shook her head. "Nothing."

He put his hand on his hips, and she tried to smile but it came out more like a grimace.

"Tell me the truth."

"It's my mom," Imari replied. "She wasn't all that happy with me, but what else is new?"

Zephyr shook his head and pulled her into a hug. "Ah, Imari, when are you going to just block her?"

She laid her head on his shoulder. "She is the only family I have left."

Abruptly, there was the sound of paper rustling, and they both turned to see her cat's head ducking inside Zephyr's bag. Thankfully, the coffee was still intact.

"Why don't you get dressed?" He quickly darted over to shoo the disgruntled cat away and pick up the two cups. "And I will feed the menace."

Imari nodded and forced a smile. "Okay."

She took a deep breath. Her heart still ached from her mother's words. But Imari had long practiced shoving those emotions deep down. It was the only way Imari could deal with her mother.

Imari sighed and headed to the bathroom to get ready for the day.

Hours later, Imari watched the crowd. The coffee and danish that Zephyr had bought her were long gone. She turned to see Zephyr excitedly explaining the meaning of a fall landscape painting to a gorgeous Asian man.

His face was alight with joy, he waved his hands animatedly. The man wasn't even looking at the painting. His eyes were glued to Zephyr. And Imari could understand why. No matter where they went, Zephyr was always the center of attention. He was tall, with a willowy build and golden-brown skin.

His short, curly hair constantly fell into his eyes, while his neatly trimmed beard only added to his androgynous appeal.

Imari shook her head and turned around to stare pointedly back at the crowd.

The town square of the small hamlet of Appeley had turned into an ocean of white tents. Each tent had something special. There were typical harvest fruits and veggies for sale: pumpkins, squash, beets, corn, and, of course, with this being the apple festival, apples. Yet there were also arts and crafts.

Directly across from Zephyr's tents was a display of adorable corn dolls. People milled from tent to tent, country music blasting over the speakers.

This would be exciting if she wasn't stuck in this cold tent.

Imari was freezing and bored. The first few hours she was happy to people-watch and play on her phone. But now, she just wanted to go home or to any place that was warm. It was November, and usually, in this part of Texas, there was still some residual summer heat.

This year, a cold front came early.

Finally, Zephyr took down the painting and brought it to the front. Imari rang the man up, and she didn't miss him handing Zephyr his card. After he left, Zephyr punched the air.

"This makes the third sale of the day."

"Your charm is impressive." Imari nodded and gestured to the card.

"Hey! Elliot just likes my art."

Imari lifted an eyebrow.

Zephyr huffed indignantly, "I'm an excellent artist."

Imari giggled, "You really are."

Her eyes gazed around the various paintings. Zephyr was truly talented. He mostly painted landscapes that were so lifelike, they could almost be photographs. The colors were always vibrant hues of orange, brown, red, green, and gold. They practically popped off the canvas. You could almost feel that you were standing at the height of the Hill Country.

Zephyr was exactly the type who loved to hike into the depths of the forests surrounding Appeley and paint for hours. Hell, he admitted this was the reason he'd moved there in the first place.

And even though drawing was part of Imari's job as a graphic designer, she still envied her best friend's talents.

"Earth to Imari." Zephyr waved in front of her face.

"Oh, sorry," Her cheeks flushed red. She stood up. "I'm hungry, and I could use another coffee."

Zephyr nodded, "Same."

Zephyr wanted some vegan sliders and tater twisters from Bobbie Jean's diner, which had its own booth at the festival. After Zephyr gave her some directions, Imari was off. The town's core was packed full of people. Not only did most residents of Appeley show up to this event, but plenty of people came from the surrounding areas as well. Imari stood on her tiptoes, but she couldn't see the pumpkin stand Zephyr told her to turn right at.

"Damn it," Imari cursed under her breath. "I hate being so short."

With a resigned sigh, Imari walked around, looking for any hint of the pumpkin stand. The festival area was small and she would find Bobbie Jean's booth sooner or later, right? For a while, Imari walked aimlessly, annoyed at being jostled and pushed by the crowd.

"Great, I'm lost," Imari muttered to herself. She was just about to ask the nearest vendor for directions when someone shoved her hard. Imari felt herself falling forward into what she was sure was going to be a painful collision with the ground when abruptly, a pair of powerful arms caught her.

"Are you okay?"

Imari looked up to meet almond-shaped brown eyes so dark that they shone like polished river stones. Imari gasped as she took in the woman's face. She thought she was used to being around beautiful people. Hell, Zephyr was her best friend, after all.

But this woman was on another level. She was tall, with a tight swimmer's build. She had dark umber skin a few shades deeper than Imari's. Her savior had long black hair that was pulled up into a sloppy bun to show off a neat fade underneath.

Imari's eyes couldn't help but dart down to the fullest lips she had ever seen. She licked her lips and then darted her head up to see those eyes get impossibly darker and hot enough to burn.

Cheeks warming in embarrassment, Imari stumbled back, "Um, sorry."

The woman snapped out of her daze, and then she frowned. "Do I know you?"

Imari shook her head. "I don't think so."

'I definitely would have remembered seeing someone like you,' She thought to herself.

"Imari?" She looked Imari up and down. And Imari barely repressed another shiver. "Imari Haines?

Imari blinked in amazement. "Yes?"

The woman laughed. "I knew I recognized your face!"

"What?"

The woman quirked an eyebrow. "You remember me, don't you?"

"I'm sorry?" Imari squeaked.

"My family used to go to the same church? Our mothers were friends." She gave a low chuckle. "You used to always steal Mr. Haversham's begonias to make flower crowns."

Then, everything clicked: a memory of a pretty little girl with a brilliant smile. A smile that was achingly similar to the one this woman was giving Imari right now.

"Cassidy?" Imari clutched her chest. "Cassidy Martinez?!"

There, standing in the sunlight, thousands of miles away from Houston, was her childhood best friend: who was familiar, strange, and utterly devastating.

Chapter Two

To bend with apples the moss'd cottage-trees,
And fill all fruit with ripeness to the core;
To swell the gourd, and plump the hazel shells
With a sweet kernel; to set budding more,
— **To Autumn by John Keats**

"I can't believe that it's you."

Imari could only nod because she, in an instant, felt that the real world had turned sideways into a dream. "I-" she stuttered, shaking her head.

"I promise to write every day," Cassidy promised.

Imari wiped the tears off of her face. She stubbornly set her chin. "You promise?"

"We are going to be friends forever." Cassidy stuck out her pinky finger. "I promise."

Imari hooked her pinky finger under Cassidy, "Forever"

The memory faded from her mind's eye, and instead of the lanky child in dirty overalls, the gorgeous woman was standing before her today.

"W-what are you doing here?" Imari spluttered, stepping back.

"I live here. Moved to town five years ago," Cassidy chuckled. "Are you down here for the festival?"

Imari shook her head. "No, I just moved to Appeley."

Cassidy's eyes went wide. "No way! Why haven't I seen you around?"

"Hey!" Imari shouted, when she shoved again into her childhood best friend.

Cassidy was distractingly close, the heat of her body seeping into her. And my god, the woman smelled amazing. She smelled of coffee, cinnamon, and something that reminded her of fresh pumpkin pie straight out of the oven.

Cassidy's arms went around Imari's waist. "Are you okay?" her mouth was only inches from Imari's ear. The rich, smooth alto made Imari shiver.

"I'm fine," Imari stuttered and quickly stepped back. She looked away, her cheeks warm. Imari had to get a grip on herself. She took a deep breath and tried to figure out the swiftest course to Bobbie's Jeans, or hell, she would settle for a way back to Zephyr's tent.

Cassidy smiled. "You're lost, aren't you?"

"Yeah," Imari finally admitted, defeated. "Do you know how to find Bobbie Jean's tent?"

"Yeah, it's on the other side of the fair."

"I know. I should have asked for directions earlier."

"Lucky for you," Cassidy said. "I'm on my way to Bobbie Jean's as well." Her childhood friend offered her an arm, and Imari felt her heart pound rapidly. 'Is she flirting with me?' She was being silly. Cassidy was just being friendly, but Imari slipped her arm through Cassidy's and followed her lead through the press of the crowd.

"So, how have you been?"

Cassidy shrugged. "I can't complain. My life was pretty boring after Houston. Graduated high school, went to U.T. Austin, moved down here, and opened a business."

"That's not boring." Imari shook her head.

"Well, it's far from an exciting life of traveling the world and uncovering ancient artifacts."

Imari laughed, "I forgot you wanted to be Indiana Jones."

Cassidy playfully shoved her. "I was pretty disillusioned by the time I graduated. Being an anthropologist wasn't as fun as I thought it would be.."

"Really?" Imari asked as she remembered how many "expeditions" they both went on as kids. Her favorite expedition was finding the holy grail that was hidden conveniently near the pecan tree in Cassidy's backyard. They had so much fun digging it up, knee-deep in dirt, and not caring a lick that Imari's mother was going to be pissed that she dirtied her dress.

"Yeah." Cassidy shrugged. "What about you? Did you become a famous artist?"

"No," Imari shook her head. "I'm a freelance designer."

Cassidy lifted an eyebrow. "That's pretty cool."

"My mother wouldn't say that."

Cassidy grimaced, "sorry."

"My mom hasn't changed all that much," Imari replied, bitterly. Her mind wandered back to the conversation she had with her mother that morning. She shook her head and changed the subject. Imari spotted the pumpkin stand, and they both turned the corner.

"So, what are you doing now? You said you moved down here five years ago?"

"Yeah, I came down here and opened a coffee shop."

"Really?" Imari asked, surprised. There were only a few coffee shops in town, and she was too lazy to go further than the Starbucks a block away from her apartment. "Which one?"

"Topped Off."

Imari nearly tripped over her shoes, but thankfully caught herself. She had been clumsy enough for the day.

"Topped off?!" Imari asked, stopping in the middle of the crowd. "Zephyr's favorite place?"

"You know Zeph?"

"Yeah, he's my best friend."

Cassidy shook her head ruefully. "Wow, what a small world! Zephyr and I have been friends for a while. He's a regular at my coffee shop."

Imari nodded. "Yeah, he swears by your macchiatos."

She smelled the food before she saw Bobbie Jean's tent. It smelled divine. Of course, Imari could smell roasting turkey legs, but beneath there was a mixture of smells that made Imari's stomach rumble. She absently rubbed her belly in the vain hope that it would stop making such embarrassing noises.

"Hungry?" Cassidy asked, grinning.

"Oh, shut up," Imari said, as they both got into line.

The queue was long, but they passed the time catching up. Imari had tons of questions, but she didn't know how to ask. Eventually, things fell into a long, awkward silence. Imari couldn't stop looking at Cassidy. She was afraid that this was some strange daydream and her friend would simply disappear. Finally, they could order their food.

"Well, well, ain't it my competition," said Bobbie Jean. Bobbie Jean was a fat, white woman in her late to mid-50s with long, ginger hair sprinkled with gray that twisted into a topknot that had tendrils escaping to frame her cheerful, round face.

"Oh, don't be like that," Cassidy chuckled. "You know damn well you make the best apple pie in the state."

Bobbie Jean wagged a wooden spoon at Cassidy. "And don't you forget it."

Cassidy laughed, and Bobbie turned to throw a sly grin at Imari. "And here you are with the newbie. You sure don't waste any time."

Imari spluttered, her cheeks hot with embarrassment.

"Oh, you stop it, you old busybody," Cassidy chided.

She sighed and put her hands on her hips. "Fine, now what will y'all want?"

They quickly ordered, and in no time at all, Cassidy's and Imari's hands were full of food.

"Let me walk you back to your booth."

"Um, okay," Imari agreed. "But I don't know where it is?"

"Do you remember which booths were next to yours?"

Imari thought about it for a moment and said, "Someone was selling corn dolls, and I think the next booth was selling handmade thanksgiving themed figurines."

Cassidy threw her a look. "Yeah, I know where that is. Follow me."

They both juggled the food into their arms, making sure they got a secure grip on their individual containers. Imari and Cassidy walked side by side through the throng of people. And for a moment, it was like old times.

The two women walked in silence for a few moments when Cassidy blurted out: "What made you move way out here?"

Imari answered, biting her lip. "I love Houston, but I needed a change." That was an understatement, but she couldn't quite say: '*I ran away from home after leaving my fiancée at the altar,*' could she?

"Yeah, I can understand that," Cassidy replied ruefully. "The pace down here is slower than Austin. It's a nice change."

"Yeah," Imari nodded. There was something about Appeley that instantly made her feel at home. She always thought small towns would be full of closed-minded people who would judge her for not being a god-fearing straight girl. Yet her loud and flamboyant best friend thrived in this town. He wasn't looked down on and wasn't the subject of sneers and gossip.

Appeley just accepted him happily into their fold. And to her surprise, they welcomed Imari just the same.

It had been a pleasant change from the way people treated her at church and in her old neighborhood.

Cassidy turned to give her a wide grin that made Imari's heart sped up in her chest. "Well, I'm glad I bumped into you."

Imari bit her lip and tried to ignore the fact that once again this woman was making her blush again.

Imari and Cassidy fell into a comfortable conversation as they made their way back. It was like no time had passed at all, and they were back in the third ward, sitting on her parent's porch.

Yet, this version of her best friend was both familiar and an enigma that Imari couldn't help but long to figure out. Cassidy's eyes lit up as she talked about her business and how hard she worked to get it off the ground or when she spoke about the friends, she made in town and her weekend road trips on her Yamaha.

Imari talked about home, all while making sure that she didn't trip into the minefield that was her family and her abrupt breakup. Instead, she talked about how she liked Appeley, her job, her adventures with Zephyr, and even her cat.

Before Imari knew it, they were once again at Zephyr's booth, and Imari couldn't help but feel disappointed. As they approached, Zephyr's face broke into a wide grin. He jumped up and took the food out of Imari's hands.

"Hey, Mari. I see you picked up a stray."

Cassidy smirked.

"I got lost and bumped into Cassidy." Imari blushed. "She was kind enough to offer to walk me back."

Cassidy threw her a smile. "Besides, we are old friends. Isn't that right, Imari?"

Imari nodded, and Zephyr only gave a knowing smirk. "Friends, huh?"

Imari wished she could wipe that look off of his face. Instead, she gave him a quelling look that absolutely did nothing to erase that smug grin off his face.

"Cassidy!"

The three of them turned to see another Latina woman with short, wavy hair coming up to them, waving.

"Hey, Peyton!" Cassidy waved back. Imari felt a sudden churning in her stomach as she looked at the two of them.Was it asking for way too much for someone like Cassidy to be single?

This Peyton woman looked so good right next to Cassidy. She was everything that Imari wasn't: pretty, thin, and younger than Imari. She pursed her lips and tried to ignore the attraction to Cassidy and what she refused to admit was jealousy gnawing at her insides.

Peyton smiled at her. "I have been looking all over for you."

Cassidy groaned, "What's broken now?"

Peyton rolled her eyes. "The espresso machine, and the crowd is getting restless." She turned to Imari and grinned. "Hey, you are Imari, right? Zephyr talks about you all the time."

Imari pasted on a smile. "Yeah." She threw a bewildered look at a very amused Zephyr.

Zephyr waved at Peyton. "Hey, what's up? Are you here to buy art? "

"Nope." Peyton shook her head. "Got to retrieve the boss."

Cassidy ruefully shook her head. "The reason I can't get a moment's peace at the shop."

Imari's eyes went wide. Maybe Peyton and Cassidy weren't together? Imari couldn't help but hope they were just co-workers?

Zephyr nodded to Peyton. "My friend here is the best barista on this side of Austin."

Peyton snorted, "You are such a charmer."

Zephyr's smirk widened impossibly wider. "Are you coming to this week's D&D game?"

"Yep! Wouldn't miss it. I got this new Dragonborn character that I created—"

Cassidy coughed and threw Imari an apologetic look. "We better get going before they dive headlong into geek talk."

Imari's shoulders slumped because she didn't want Cassidy to go. She bit her lip. "Can I have your phone?" Imari blurted out. The others looked at her, and Imari wanted to sink into the floor.

"S-so we can hang out sometime?" Imari squeaked.

Cassidy grinned and handed Imari her phone. With shaking fingers, Imari quickly put her number in Cassidy's phone.

"I'll talk to you later," Cassidy waved, "Don't be a stranger, okay?"

Cassidy handed the food to Peyton, and they both walked away, joining in the crowd. Yet Imari couldn't quite pry her eyes from the woman's retreating back. She was not at all staring at Cassidy's delectable bubble butt. No siree, nothing to see here, move along.

Imari jumped when Cassidy suddenly turned back and caught her eyes. The other woman's mouth splitting into a wide, delighted grin. Peyton said something, but at this distance, Imari couldn't hear before they both finally disappeared into the crowd.

Zephyr cackled as soon as they were out of earshot. "You gave me so much shit earlier about Elliot, and then you left me here all on my lonesome to pick up chicks."

Imari slapped him playfully on the arm. "I didn't. I told you we just bumped into each other."

"Uh, huh," Zephyr said as they both walked into the booth. "That's what they're calling it now?"

"Zephyr, stop it." Imari shrugged. "She's someone I used to know. We are basically strangers now. Hell, I don't know if she is even into girls."

Zephyr stopped and turned to stare at her. "Girl, are you kidding? The way she was eye-fucking you …"

"She wasn't interested," Imari said stubbornly, opening her own food. "Besides, I just wanted to connect with an old friend."

Zephyr sighed and put his hand on hers. "Mari, you deserve to be happy."

Imari looked down at their hands. "I know that."

"Do you?" He asked softly.

"It's way too soon to get into another relationship," Imari said, shaking her head. "And besides, Cassidy is just a friend."

"Look, I will not push this further, but I want you to consider that maybe you're selling yourself short."

Imari nodded, and silence fell as they ate their food. Yet Zephyr's words kept spinning around and around in her head.

Chapter Three

And still more, later flowers for the bees,
Until they think warm days will never cease,
For summer has o'er-brimm'd their clammy cells.
— To Autumn by John Keats

THREE DAYS LATER, IMARI STARED AT HER MONITOR. Her graphic pen tapped idly on her desk. She groaned and put her head in her hands. She needed to work, and she had to work on the rebranding project for a small multimedia company. The due date was steadily creeping up on her.

Imari jumped as there was suddenly a thump and a crash. She looked up to see Bramble sitting on top of her graphic tablet. Her sketchbook and colored pencils lay on the floor.

"Bad kitty." Imari shook her fingers at Bramble, who just stared at her for a long moment, and then pointedly licked his paw.

With a put-upon sigh, Imari got up, picked up the items off the floor, and put them neatly back on her desk.

Imari gave Bramble the attention he demanded by giving him a few scritches before she stretched. She went to the windows and looked out into the woods that surrounded her apartment complex.

The sky was gray and dismal, the colorful autumn trees swaying violently in the breeze. Imari took out her phone and checked her messages.

Imari's fingers paused over them. Most messages were from her mother. She clicked inside the text chain and winced.

Mom: Call Me.

Mom: It's been two days and you are still sulking?

Mom: Call me right now, Imari.

Mom: You are ignoring me now?

Mom: You don't pick up your phone, you ignore my messages. It's like you don't love me.

Her fingers started to type, and then she deleted it. Because honestly, what could Imari say that would satisfy her mother? Her mother would treat her like shit and then guilt Imari into not cutting her off. It had been a cycle they had been going through since college.

Imari's fingers hovered over the block button, but in the end, she just ignored it and exited it out of her mother's text chain altogether. Imari scrolled down, and her fingers hovered over Cassidy's number.

She clicked into the messages and found only a single "Hey."

Imari had been trying to figure out what to say to her. Imari was worrying about her sudden inability to send even a simple text message these days. She groaned. Talking to Cassidy had been so easy, but then she had caught Imari staring at her ass.

The other woman didn't seem to mind, but Imari was still embarrassed.

Imari shoved her phone back into her pocket. She felt so out of her depth. And what if Zephyr had been wrong? What if Imari had been imagining things?

Imari groaned and slapped her forehead.

Bramble meowed, and Imari spun on her heel. "No more knocking down my stuff!" She wagged her finger at the cat, who just knocked down yet another book.

Imari threw up her hands and quickly shoved on her coat, grabbed her keys, and headed out of her apartment.

Imari stared at the converted two-story brick store-front with a sign in neat calligraphy that said '*Topped Off*' with a steaming coffee mug illustration beneath it.

She walked into the coffee shop and immediately regretted her decision.

It was three o'clock in the afternoon and way past the afternoon rush. Inside, a few people were sitting at dark wooden tables. Some talked quietly amongst themselves, while one typed on a laptop and a person in the corner read a newspaper.

Her palms are sweaty and her heart pounding in her chest. Imari thought she was going to throw up. She was damn nervous. Maybe she could leave now before anyone saw her?

"Imari, right?"

Imari turned to see Peyton coming up to her, holding a tray. Imari waved awkwardly at the other woman.

"Hey," Imari replied as she went to the register, which sat on a long, dark walnut counter.

"You here for the coffee or the boss?" Peyton asked, blue eyes dancing with mischief.

"Um—" Imari didn't know what to say at Peyton's bluntness. No wonder Zephyr and Peyton were such good friends. They were cut from the same cloth.

"Let me go get the boss—"

Imari opened her mouth to protest, but Peyton was already darting away and heading past the shelves that had bags of coffee beans and cappuccino machines to a narrow door just off the register.

'*You are in for it now*,' Imari chided herself.

Imari sighed and looked up at the chalkboard menu that hung above the shelves. She really should just leave, but as if on cue, there was a roar of thunder that made her jump. Imari turned, mouth open, to see the sky finally open and pour down rain.

Imari gave a resigned sigh. She looked up at the chalkboard menu again. She threw a longing look at the door, but as if to spite her, it rained harder.

'*Great, just great.*'

The door opened, and Cassidy walked out of the room with Peyton close on her heels. Cassidy's mouth split into a grin. "Well, well, I thought I scared you off."

"Sorry, I was just swamped at work."

And it certainly wasn't because Imari was too scared that she would make a total and complete fool out of herself in front of this gorgeous woman who she wanted to climb like a tree.

A smile tugged at the edge of Cassidy's lips.

'*That smile should be classified as a dangerous weapon*,' she thought to herself a bit hysterically.

The doorbell rang as a customer hurried inside, obviously trying to escape the downpour. Peyton smirked at both of them before she went to take the customer's order. Cassidy leaned her elbows on the counter, which showed off her tight muscular forearms.

Imari quickly looked away.

"What can I get you?"

"A cinnamon maple latte, please," Imari asked.

Cassidy grinned. "Ooh, one of my favorites. For here or to go?"

Imari threw another look at the rain and shook her head. "Definitely for here."

"Alright, one cinnamon maple latte, coming right up."

Imari waited, watching as Cassidy deftly put together her order. She couldn't take her eyes off her. Imari thought she had exaggerated how beautiful Cassidy had become. Yet, there was something so attractive about how confident she was in what was her element.

"There you go," Cassidy said, as she handed Imari her order. The smell of cinnamon was so heavenly, but as Imari took her coffee, her heart felt like it was going to pound right out of her chest.

"Thanks." Imari coughed. "How much do I owe you?"

Cassidy chuckled, "It's on the house."

"No," Imari put down the cup and went for her purse. "Let me pay."

Imari looked up at Peyton's laughter. "Imari, you better take the offer, since Cassidy rarely gives freebies." Her mouth split into a gleeful grin as she threw a knowing look at her boss. "She must like you a lot."

Cassidy slapped her forehead and groaned. "Go do something productive, you menace, before I fire you."

Peyton rolled her eyes. "You are going to miss me when I finally graduate college."

Cassidy playfully nudged her. "But then I can get you out of my shop, and I will only see you when I need to submit my taxes."

"Haha," Peyton stuck her tongue out. "You know the customers love me more. You won't last a month without me."

Cassidy shook her head, and the doorbell rang as a couple walked through the door.

Cassidy just laughed. But if Imari hadn't been paying attention, she would have missed the look of sadness that flashed quickly on the other woman's face before she replaced it with a calm smile.

Imari wondered again if Cassidy had feelings for Peyton. It would just be her luck that someone as gorgeous as Cassidy had their sights on someone else.

Another customer walked through the door, breaking the strange moment. Imari, seeing that it was her opportunity to flee, picked up her cup and said, "Thanks."

Then she scuttled to a table in the back.

Imari quickly sat her drink down. She opened her purse and pulled out her old, battered copy of her favorite Beverly Jenkins novel, and tried to ignore the pounding of her heart.

Imari removed the receipt that she had used as a bookmark and peaked up behind the open paperback to see if Cassidy was still looking at her.

Cassidy was gone, and Peyton was back manning the register alone. Imari's shoulders slumped. She felt both disappointed and relieved. Imari was just projecting her feelings on Cassidy. Her old friend was just being nice, wasn't she? But the way Cassidy looked at her, the way her long fingers lingered when they touched... Imari was so confused.

With a put-upon sigh, Imari's eyes went back to her book. At first, she couldn't pay attention. Cassidy was a constant thought in her mind. A part of her was disappointed Cassidy had left.

Even though she didn't have a chance with her old friend, Cassidy was nice to look at.

Sighing again, she put her attention firmly back on her book, and to her surprise, she could eventually sink into the familiar world of 'Rebel'. She bit her lip as she read, so caught up in Drake and Valinda's exploits that she didn't hear anyone approach.

"Can I sit here?"

Imari jerked, almost knocking over her empty mug. Luckily, Imari could catch it in time. She looked up to see Cassidy standing in front of her with a sheepish look on her face.

"I'm so sorry. I didn't mean to startle you."

Imari blushed, quickly putting her book away. "No, it's okay." She gestured to the chair. "Sure."

Cassidy slid into the chair across from her. "So, what were you reading?"

Imari shrugged. "Just some historical fiction?"

Cassidy lit up, "Really? What about?"

"Post-Civil War."

"My focus in college was the Civil War."

Imari bit her lip. "It's historical romance." She took out the book and showed Cassidy the cover. "I don't think that would be your cup of tea."

"Can I see it?"

Imari reluctantly nodded, and Cassidy took the book out of her hand and examined the cover and the back blurb. "You're right, this is not usual reading."

Imari went rigid, waiting for Cassidy to make fun of her like everyone else when they found out that Imari loved to read romance novels. Yet, none of the ridicule came, just a thoughtful look.

"I'll add it to my reading list."

Imari shook her head. "You don't have to pretend that you like it-"

Cassidy gave her a soft smile. "No, you always had the best taste, and I—" She coughed and looked back down at the book. "I trust your judgment."

It warmed her to the core that Cassidy was actually interested and would even consider it.

"So you studied the Civil War in college?"

"Yeah." Cassidy shrugged. "I always thought it was boring. You remember Mr. Finley's history class?"

Imari laughed. "He had the worst monotone voice."

Cassidy nodded. "Yeah, but once I got to college, I was interested in all the nuances of the war. In particular, the Black soldiers on both sides of the war."

Imari listened as Cassidy excitedly talked about her time at college and her classes. It was clear that the passion for history she had as a child had only grown with time. Imari found herself telling Cassidy about her own time at Southwestern University, including meeting Zephyr in her freshmen year and bonding over both of them being bisexual.

"I wish I was still tight with my college friends." Cassidy shook her head. "But most of them moved out of the state."

"Zephyr has been the only person in college I still talk to." Imari shrugged. "I'm so lucky to have him in my life. He's come through for me."

Imari thought about how he had been the only one to be on her side after everything blew up in

Houston. How he begged her to move down here to Appeley.

"How long have you and Peyton been together?" Imari blurted out. She gasped and put a hand to her mouth. Oh god, she didn't ask that?

There was a long, awkward silence before Cassidy laughed. Imari clenched her eyes shut, her cheeks hot with embarrassment.

"I'm sorry for laughing." Cassidy coughed and composed herself. "Imari."

Imari refused to look up.

Cassidy sighed, "Imari, please look at me."

Imari inwardly fought with herself for a long moment before she hesitantly looked up.

"Peyton is just my friend. We are not dating." Cassidy shook her head. "I think we would end up killing each other if we dated."

"But — "Imari bit her lip. "You looked so sad when you talked about her leaving you."

"I was sad because Peyton was right. Peyton is way more likable than me. When she's gone, I'm going to have to actually talk to my customers." Cassidy shrugged. "It's not something I'm good at."

"Can I ask you a question?"

Imari bit her lip and nodded.

"Would it be too forward to ask you out on a date?"

Imari's eyes went wide as she stared at Cassidy in shock and amazement.

"There is going to be a Movie in the Park thing on Sunday," Cassidy said. "Would you like to go?"

Imari's first instinct was to enthusiastically say yes, but then was it too soon after her breakup with Todd? It had only been three months. Was she ready to date again? And with a woman to boot? Especially since she hadn't dated a girl since her junior year of college.

Cassidy looked away and coughed. "If you don't want to go—"

Imari reached over and took her hand. "I want to go, but I think there is something you should know."

Cassidy looked up at her and squeezed her hand back. "You can tell me anything."

'Am I *really going to tell her this?*' Imari thought to herself.

What did her past matter to Cassidy? No one in this town, except for Zephyr, knew the real reason she moved here. She was a stranger here. It was a relief to no longer be the center of gossip.

"Imari?"

Imari bit her lip. She was torn: would Cassidy think worse of her if Imari told her the truth? She took a deep breath, "I just got out of a long-term relation-ship," Imari sighed. "And the breakup was messy."

Cassidy nodded. "I can understand. I had a few messy breakups in the past."

Imari winced. "Yeah, well, I don't think you left your fiancé at the altar."

Cassidy's eyes went wide.

Imari looked down at her hands and sighed. "I never meant for that to get so out of hand." She sighed. "Todd and I were together for five years, and everyone was pressuring us to get married." She gave a bitter chuckle. "My mother disapproved that we were "living in sin". I think Todd proposed out of obligation more than love for me."

Cassidy took her hand and squeezed.

"Everything just got out of hand, and my mother was overjoyed." Imari shrugged. "For the first time in my life, my mom was proud of me." It surprised her that Cassidy wasn't running away as fast as she could. Yet, her childhood friend only looked at her with compassion.

"By the time I realized I was making a mistake; I was walking down the aisle."

Imari felt her eyes prick with tears as guilt twisted her gut. Todd didn't deserve what happened to him. He had been an innocent bystander in her family drama. Her ex didn't deserve to be humiliated in front of both their family and friends. Ultimately, Imari felt that breaking up had been the best in the end, but the way she did it?

Imari inwardly sighed. *'Todd had deserved better than that.'*

"I understand if you don't want to date me now." Imari finally said.

Cassidy's fingers tightened around hers, and she shook her head. "Thank you for trusting me enough to tell me." She met Imari's eyes. "I agree, it was a shitty thing to do."

Imari wilted on herself.

"But we all make mistakes," Cassidy said.

Imari sat up and finally met Cassidy's eyes. She could only give the other woman a weak smile in return.

"I still want to go out with you." Cassidy brushed her thumb over Imari's knuckles. "I want you to promise one thing."

"And what's that?"

"To be honest with me. If you feel uncomfortable or if you only want to be just friends, tell me."

Imari vehemently nodded.

Cassidy took her hand and kissed the knuckles. She gave Imari a slow, sexy smile that made her feel weak in the knees. "Then I'll see you on Sunday at six o'clock."

Chapter Four

Who hath not seen thee oft amid thy store?
Sometimes whoever seeks abroad may find
Thee sitting careless on a granary floor,
Thy hair soft-lifted by the winnowing wind;
— To Autumn by John Keats

"Absolutely not," Imari said, crossing her arms.

"What?" Zephyr asked as he held up a very revealing halter top.

Imari pinched her nose and suddenly remembered why she always tried to get out of shopping with Zephyr. He was her best friend, but Zephyr's idea of style and hers were incompatible.

He huffed and put the dress back on the rack. Imari rubbed her temples and looked around the clothing store. This place was one of the few places that carried her size in the mall, but honestly, she wouldn't be caught dead in most of these clothes.

"I think we should go somewhere else?"

Zephyr frowned. "Why?"

"Because I'm a thirty-year-old fat woman that is way too grown to be in a place like this."

Zephyr scoffed, "You are a 30-year-old woman who dresses like a grandma."

Zephyr and Imari glared at each other. A call broke their standoff up. Imari felt the dread pull in the pit of her stomach at the familiar ringtone. She pulled out her phone, and there was her mother.

'Of course, she would call right now.'

Imari took the phone out with a sigh and then yelped as Zephyr snatched her phone from her fingers and pressed the Decline button.

"What—"

Zephyr shook his head. "You can't let her ruin this too."

Imari groaned because she was really in for it now. Although, after her disastrous idea of telling her mother that she wasn't going to Thanksgiving over email, this was just going to make everything that much worse.

Her mother was going to start with guilt. She could hear the familiar reframe now in her head:

'I give you a wonderful home over your head, food in your stomach, clothes on your back, paid for your education, and you do me this way? Do you know how

much I sacrificed to make sure you went to your fancy private school and college?'

And the truth was, her mother sacrificed a lot to make sure she succeeded. Yet, it all came with strings attached.

"Zeph—" Imari rubbed her forehead. "You can't do things like that—"

Zephyr shook his head and slid her phone into his jeans pockets. "You just know that she is going to ruin it. She always does."

And the thing was, Zephyr was right. Her mother was constantly putting her down. Nothing could ever please her. Imari would try to help around the house, and nothing was clean enough. If Imari cooked a meal, there was always something off. And don't get Imari started on schoolwork. Imari could have A+ on all of her subjects and still hear how Mrs. Johnson's son down the street was in all AP classes or was taking early college admissions.

The less said about her mother's passive-aggressive comments on her weight, the fact she took so long to get married, or her single status now, the better.

Imari looked down and rubbed her eyes.

"You deserve to move on to someone who makes you happy." Zephyr stepped forward and put a hand on her shoulder while looking her straight in the eye. "I have never seen you look at anyone the way you look at Cassidy."

Her mind went back to the coffee shop and the way Cassidy's face lit up at things that she was interested in. Her swagger and how good Cassidy felt pressed close to her. The way her dark eyes would look at Imari.

"You are doing it again."

Imari coughed and looked away. "Doing what?"

"You got a soppy smile on your face."

Imari wanted to protest, but she could feel her mouth curving into a grin. And yes, the way Cassidy made her feel differed totally from Todd.

Being with Todd had been like putting on a comfortable old sweater that she had long outgrown. Yet, Todd never made her heart speed up as Cassidy did with just a single look. Never made her feel like anything was possible if she just jumped off the precipice.

"Mari—" Zephyr started as Imari looked at him. "I just want you to be happy and I think Cassidy can make you happy. I don't want your mom to spoil that."

Imari took a deep breath and nodded. "Okay."

Zephyr bounced on his toes, his mouth splitting into a wide, excited grin. "Great!" Zephyr whirled around and resumed going through the racks, pulling a few things.

"Here–" Zephyr shoved the pile of clothes in her arms. "Try those on."

"You must be joking—" Imari said as she spotted a blouse that was absolutely out of her comfort zone.

"Trust me."

Imari rolled her eyes and gave a long, resigned sigh before marching into the dressing room.

She quickly got dressed in the clothes Zephyr had picked out and looked into the mirror. She pursed her lips, tugging at the blouse. Imari felt exposed. The cut of the blouse showed way too much of her ample cleavage. It tied around her waist, showing off her curves.

The white contrasted nicely with her dark brown skin, but the light wash skinny jeans were tight enough to be a second skin.

Imari fiddled with her afro and felt like she was suddenly playing a part they did not prepare her for.

Zephyr knocked on the door. "Are you going to hide in there all day?"

Imari threw her reflection another look and, with a put-upon sigh, she reluctantly opened the dressing room door and stepped out.

Zephyr gave her a smug grin. "Damn, you are going to knock Cassidy off her feet."

Imari looked down and frowned. "I think it's a bit much."

Zephyr's eyes were lit with unholy glee. "Girl, trust me. Cassidy is going to love it."

"Jesus," Cassidy swore, nearly tripping over her feet as Imari made her way across the parking lot. Imari shivered as Cassidy's eyes raked up and down her body.

Imari couldn't help but notice as she approached Cassidy that the other woman's dark eyes kept lingering on back up to her cleavage. It made her both want to immediately close her jacket and to preen under the other woman's frank appreciation.

"You are so goddamn beautiful."

Imari ducked her head, her cheeks warming. "Um, thank you." She coughed and tried to ignore the way the look in Cassidy's eyes made heat spread through her.

Her gaze went to the sleek, black Yamaha motorcycle standing next to Cassidy. It had a medium size box attached to both sides of the saddle.

"This is your bike?"

"Yeah?" Cassidy replied. "This is Sable."

Imari finally looked back at Cassidy with wide eyes and snorted. "You named your motorcycle, Sable?"

Cassidy shrugged. "It's a good name." She petted Sable like someone would pet a favored horse.

Imari looked at the motorcycle and bit her lip. "I never rode a motorcycle before."

Cassidy turned to her. "You don't have to be scared."

Imari squared her chin and threw the other woman a determined look. "I'm not scared."

Cassidy gave her a pleased smile and pulled out a motorcycle helmet. "It's going to mess up your hair, though."

Imari took it and shrugged. "It's okay." She put the helmet on, and Cassidy walked over to adjust the straps. Her fingers on her skin were driving Imari crazy.

"There," Cassidy said, taking a step back and turning to get on the motorcycle. Despite her earlier bravado, Imari cautiously sat behind her date.

Then she yelped in surprise as the engine turned on, and the motor gave a loud growl.

Imari took her hands and tentatively put them around Cassidy's waist. Cassidy looked back and gave a low chuckle. "You gotta hold on tighter than that, Mari."

She gasped as Cassidy took her hands and pulled her closer to her, wrapping Imari's arms around her stomach.

Then they were off, zooming out of her apartment's parking lot and down the long road into town. The thick fall foliage was on either side of them as the brisk autumn wind whipped around them.

She closed her eyes, squeezing Cassidy tighter than was probably comfortable. Cassidy didn't complain, and then they were taking a sharp turn.

Imari snapped open her eyes, a shout leaving her lips at the sensation.

"You alright?" Cassidy shouted over the wind.

"Yeah!" Imari nodded, and she couldn't help but grin. "I'm fine."

As they drove, Imari got used to the sensation. Once Imari got over the fear that she was going to fall off the motorcycle, Imari could admit to herself that this sensation was exhilarating, and even erotic.

There was something about the vibrations of the engine revving that reignited the sharp arousal that had faded because of her earlier fear. Cassidy being so close to her only added to her building arousal.

By the time they finally made it into town and to Braeburn park, Imari's body was buzzing with need.

Cassidy turned off the engine, and Imari just stayed there, trying to get her wits back together and get her renegade body under control.

We can't eat if we stay on Sable all day.'

Imari blushed and staggered clumsily off the motorcycle. With grace Imari was envious of, Cassidy got up and caught Imari before she could fall on her ass in her high heels.

"Careful now."

"Thanks," Imari said as she took off her helmet. Cassidy took it and put it back in the box before going to the other one. She pulled out a wicker picnic basket.

Cassidy took her free hand, and they walked into the park. It was Sunday, and the park was pretty busy. Kids were running around on the playground, screaming at the top of their lungs. A few people walked their dogs, and there were even other couples taking advantage of the beautiful day.

Imari followed Cassidy out of the main play area and into a wider clearing were, at the center, was a huge blank white projection screen.

The other moviegoers were sitting on blankets or in lawn chairs, talking amongst themselves. Cassidy took them to a space near an old elderly couple.

Cassidy sat the basket down and pulled out a red and white checkered blanket from the basket and laid it on the ground.

"Your seat awaits, my lady."

Imari chuckled and sat down. "I could have brought something."

"I wanted to spoil you," Cassidy said, as she started taking out containers. Imari's mouth was watering at the sight of so much delicious food, and it all smelled divine. Butternut squash soup, a couscous cranberry salad, and chicken sandwiches.

"Are those empanadas?"

"Yes, my mamá's recipe." Cassidy shrugged. "I remembered you used to be a fan."

Mrs. Martinez's empanadas had always been the delight of every church bake sale or get-together. Mrs. Martinez would always sneak her an extra empanada.

"I don't know if they will ever be as good."

Imari knocked her shoulders playfully with Cassidy's. "Don't cut yourself short."

Cassidy looked down, a smile on her lips as she pulled out a bottle of red wine.

"You thought of everything."

"Hey, I was the one to ask you out. I should at least show you some effort."

"Well, the least I can do is help." Imari shooed Cassidy away and took out the plates and silverware.

It was quiet then as Cassidy served Imari and then herself. Imari moaned as she took a bite of her salad. She looked up to see Cassidy staring at her mouth. Cassidy coughed and glanced away.

Imari loved Cassidy was just as affected by Imari as she was by Cassidy. Everything about this date calmed her fears.

"How was your week?" Cassidy asked.

Imari smiled, "It was pretty great." She didn't tell her that their earlier meeting at Topped Off had been the highlight of her week. Instead, Imari talked about finishing the new branding project and about shopping with Zephyr.

Cassidy told her about the new recipes she was working on and mentioned Peyton's constant harping on her about overworking, which led to a few stories about Peyton's shenanigans at the coffee shop. When Imari asked about her bike, Cassidy told her about all the work she'd put into it and a recent road trip to Austin to visit her family.

Imari couldn't help but be envious of Cassidy. She had such Cassidy a loving and uncomplicated relationship with her family. Imari was the only child, with her mother's entire hopes wrapped up in her, and she wasn't all that close to any of her extended family.

Imari put away her feelings about her family, for once taking Zephyr's advice. She was just going to just enjoy the night and see where it went.

Now, with the food done, Imari ignored Cassidy's protestations as she put away the empty containers, trash, and plates back into the basket.

The sun was just setting; the air had gotten cooler, and Imari unconsciously scooted closer as the movie started.

Chapter Five

Or on a half-reap'd furrow sound asleep,
Drows'd with the fume of poppies, while thy hook
Spares the next swath and all its twined flowers:
And sometimes like a gleaner thou dost keep
— To Autumn by John Keats

As the movie started with a voice-over talking about love in Paris, Imari tried to get comfortable as she watched the opening montage of couples kissing. Imari turned to Cassidy and saw that the other woman's attention was entirely on the movie. An old black and white film was projected on the screen and the moonlight lit Cassidy's face. Imari thought about kissing her, just scooting in and pressing her lips to Cassidy's.

She shook her head and tried to watch the movie. Yet, every time she could finally get into it, Cassidy would laugh, or she would brush against Imari and she couldn't stop turning to stare at Cassidy. The antics of Audrey Hepburn and Gary Cooper played on screen, but Imari found Cassidy's reactions much more fascinating.

Cassidy turned, and their eyes caught. The world seemed to melt away as their eyes met in the dark. All Imari could hear was her heart pounding in her ears as Cassidy smiled down at her, put her arm around her, and pulled her close.

She ducked down and pressed a soft kiss to Imari's head.

"Enjoying the movie?"

Imari nodded, but she couldn't say anything. Emotions bubbled up inside her. An emotion that was way too early to name was there too, and it terrified and delighted her all the same. Imari looked up, and Cassidy was still looking down at her. There was just something about her, about how Cassidy made her feel like they were two magnets being pulled to each other.

Imari felt like her heart was going to pound out of her chest as she leaned forward and pressed her lips to Cassidy's own, just a flutter of lips so soft that it was barely a kiss at all. Cassidy went rigid, and Imari frowned and pulled back

'Did I overstep? Am I a horrible kisser?'

Cassidy blinked, and suddenly she was taking Imari's face in her hands. Her thumb moved across her cheek, and her gaze locked on Imari's lips. Imari couldn't help but lick her lips, and Cassidy gave a soft groan and kissed her.

Imari moaned and pressed herself closer to Cassidy as her lips moved over Imari's in a slow, drugging kiss that made her toes curl. She kissed Imari like she had all the time in the world. Imari could only slide her arms around Cassidy's neck and succumb to the pleasure of her touch.

A loud cough pulled Imari back to earth. She jumped back, her face flushed as she noticed an elderly woman was looking right at them. Imari looked away.

'Oh, god I just got caught making out like I was a teenager.' Imari's cheeks flushed in embarrassment, but to both her confusion and delight, Cassidy refused to pull away.

The woman harrumphed, but her husband threw them an apologetic look. Imari ducked her head in Cassidy's shoulders.

"It's alright," Cassidy said into her hair.

Imari looked up to see that the woman's attention was back on the movie, but Imari was still embarrassed. Cassidy squeezed her shoulders, and Imari eventually just tried to let it go as she laid her head on Cassidy's shoulder.

Imari knew she could keep her distance, but she felt so safe and warm in Cassidy's arms. And Imari wasn't quite ready to let the feeling go. And so they sat in the dark, the cool autumn breeze fluttering through the trees, as they watched the movie.

Her mind kept replaying Cassidy's kiss and wondering how soon she could get Cassidy alone to do it again.

"Please make yourself at home," Imari said as she clicked on the light. She threw her keys on the coffee table. Bramble lay on the sofa as he if owned it, his multi-color tail swishing back and forth.

"Okay." Cassidy did just that as she sat down on the couch. Imari went to pet Bramble, but her cat darted from under her hand and went to rub himself against Cassidy.

'*Traitor.*' Imari thought fondly to herself.

"Let me make you some coffee," Imari said as she headed into the kitchen area. She opened the cabinets and pulled out two mugs. Before going to start the coffee, Imari turned to look at Cassidy, who was petting Bramble. The cat was eating up every inch of attention.

It was adorable.

Imari bit her lip; she still couldn't believe she'd been bold enough to invite Cassidy up to her apartment. Everyone knew that going up for coffee was an invitation for sex, and she had been turned on all night. Yet, she was still nervous. Did she want to do this? What if she was horrible at it? It had been almost a decade since she last had sex with a woman.

'I can't believe that I invited Cassidy up to my apartment.'

Yes, she used the tired old cover of inviting them up for coffee, but Cassidy had to know that she wanted to climb her like a tree. This was so out of character for Imari. She didn't even sleep with Todd until the third date.

Imari's mind flashed back to that kiss at the park, and her body throbbed with anticipation.

"Imari?"

Imari turned, and Cassidy threw her a worried look. "You okay?"

Imari nodded. "Yeah, I'm fine-"

Cassidy lifted an eyebrow and patted Bramble one last time before she stood. Her long legs quickly ate the distance between them.

"You know I don't expect anything," Cassidy said as if reading Imari's mind. She pushed a tendril of hair behind her ear. "I just really like spending time with you."

Imari bit her lip and sighed. "I really like spending time with you too." She stepped into Cassidy's arms. "But I'm just nervous."

"It's okay to be nervous," Cassidy said, "And again, we can just hang out."

Imari took a deep breath, looking up right into Cassidy's eyes. "I-I just don't want to hang out." Imari leaned forward again and kissed her. Their lips collided into a hot and demanding kiss. Imari groaned and was overwhelmed with the taste of Cassidy, something sweet and dark and hinting vaguely of cranberries. Her tongue licked into Cassidy's mouth, their tongues meeting in a sensual dance that made her body thrum with a desire so deep that it was all-consuming.

She looped her arms around Cassidy's neck and pressed flush against her. Imari's pussy was so wet. It had been for a while now. And suddenly, Cassidy's hands were slipping into her hair, gripping it, as her tongue plundered Imari's mouth. Imari ground against her, needing something to soothe her desperate need.

Cassidy broke the kiss, and Imari whimpered at the loss. Her lover didn't keep her waiting for long, her mouth nipping at Imari's chin and then licking down her neck. Cassidy's hands crept up to cup her ass.

Imari stepped back, and she jumped as there was a loud, angry yowl.

Imari looked down to see Bramble hiss at her and then scurry out of the kitchen and back into the living room.

"Is he okay?" Cassidy asked.

"Bramble will be fine," Imari shook her head. "He's probably going to be pissy about it for a while."

Cassidy ducked her head on her shoulder, shaking with laughter. "Another interruption."

Imari shook her head and ran her hand through Cassidy's long hair. "I think if we take this to the bedroom, we won't be interrupted."

Cassidy straightened up and kissed her again. "Show me."

Imari laced her fingers with Cassidy and led her into her bedroom. She pointedly locked the door, and then abruptly she was being kissed within an inch of her life. Imari sighed into Cassidy's kiss. Cassidy directed Imari backward until her body bumped into something that could only be her bed.

Imari sat down on the edge. Breaking the kiss, she untied her wrap blouse, and Cassidy put out her hands to stop her.

"Let me do that," Cassidy said, her voice low, husky. "I have been dreaming of peeling this off of you all night."

Chapter Six

How Cassidy peeled off her blouse was reverent, as if Imari were opening the best Christmas present. The blouse fell to the ground, and Cassidy dipped to kiss Imari again, her hands cupping Imari's full breasts.

Imari gasped into Cassidy's mouth as her thumbs brushed against her own already-erect nipples through her bra.

"You have been tempting me all day."

"Well, I'm glad I'm not the only one who had to suffer."

Cassidy chuckled as she reached behind Imari to free her breasts. Cassidy groaned, "I love I can barely hold them in my hand."

"A breast woman then?" Imari chuckled, feeling confident under Cassidy's lust and frank adoration.

Cassidy hummed in ascent as she dipped to take a nipple in her mouth. Imari's mouth dropped open at the sudden pleasure and the feeling of Cassidy's tongue flickering against her nipple. Every flicker traveled straight to her throbbing clit.

She slid her hand through Cassidy's hair, holding her close to her heaving chest. In response, the other woman exchanged those maddening licks for hard sucks.

Imari just held on, her hips canting against Cassidy as she suckled from her tit, and then with obscene pop, her lover went to the other one. Licking and kissing and sucking and driving her mad.

'*Were my breasts always this sensitive?*' Imari wildly thought to herself.

Cassidy finally let up, her hands squeezing and massaging Imari's breasts. "God, I love your tits."

She dipped down to the space in between them, licking a long line down onto Imari's big round stomach, every touch reverent, and Imari never felt as beautiful as she did at that moment.

When Cassidy got to her jeans, she knelt between Imari's parted thighs. Imari thought she would die from the anticipation of what would come.

"Please?" Imari whimpered, arching into Cassidy's fingers as they slid down Imari's thick thighs.

"Please what, baby?" Cassidy asked.

Imari tried to get the words past her throat. "I—" Imari whimpered as those hands slid close to the apex of her thighs. Her entrance was so wet, she'd practically soaked her panties and probably ruined her jeans too.

"Tell me what you want," Cassidy said, her voice firm.

Imari's cheeks were hot with embarrassment, but more than that, the steel in Cassidy's voice just added fuel to Imari's desire.

"I need your mouth." Imari coughed and looked away.

Cassidy stood up and leaned over to hold Imari's head in her hands. And goddamn, those eyes bored into hers. "Where do you need it, baby?"

Imari swallowed. "I need your mouth."

"Where?"

Imari closed her eyes, her cheeks still red. "Uh... my...my pussy."

Cassidy gave her a sly smile and darted down to take her mouth in a demanding kiss. "Good girl."

Cassidy's hands went to her belt. After she unbuckled it, her hands quickly undid Imari's jeans and slid both her jeans and underwear down in one pull.

Cassidy squatted back down between her legs, taking off her heels. She kissed one foot and then the other.

Imari laid back on the bed, staring down at one of the most gorgeous women she ever met down between her bare thighs.

"You are so lovely."

Cassidy spread Imari's thighs wider, leaned closer, and spread her lips.

Imari sighed as she felt Cassidy's hot breath against her aching need, her hips arching up. "Please."

Imari arched off the bed as Cassidy took a long lick across her cunt from top to the bottom. The wet, hot tongue against her felt so good. Cassidy's tongue gave a few more passes over her quivering pussy before she finally, god finally, took her clit between those sinful lips and sucked.

"God, yes."

The pleasure hit her like a tidal wave, and all Imari could do was buck against it. Cassidy grabbed her thighs and pressed her closer.

Imari groaned and tried to hold on for dear life as Cassidy just sucked around her throbbing clit. And then suddenly she felt a finger probing inside of her, and as soaked as Imari was, Cassidy's fingers slid in almost effortlessly.

Cassidy's questing fingers felt wonderful against the aching walls of her cunt. But she wanted more, and Imari was so close to coming.

"Cassidy," Imari moaned.

And then Cassidy did something with her tongue that hit that magic spot within her, and Imani's body jerked and then went rigid as she finally came.

Imari could only lay there as Cassidy finally let go of her now over-sensitive clit to dip inside of her channel, lapping at every inch of her juices like it was the finest of wine.

"Cass," Imari said, pulling her by her shoulders.

Cassidy reluctantly sat up, her face drenched in Imari's slick. Imari leaned up to kiss her. The taste of herself on Cassidy's tongue was delicious and intoxicating. She couldn't help herself from licking every bit of her juices from Cassidy's mouth and face.

Imari gave her a pleased smile. "Need anything?"

She looked away and crossed her arms to cover herself. What was Imari doing? She was never this wanton, this out of control.

"Imari?" Cassidy breathed.

Imari hesitantly turned to look at her. "Yes?"

"Are you okay?"

Imari opened her mouth and then closed it. "I'm fine. Do you want anything?"

"Only you," Cassidy said, oddly seriously. Imari shivered at the other woman's words. Cassidy's intensity still scared her. They only just reconnected for such a short time. Yet, Imari couldn't deny that she returned her lover's feelings.

Imari just kissed her instead. Trying to tell Cassidy with her lips and tongue. all of the feelings bottled up inside of her.

They broke apart, panting for breath, and with their eyes boring into each other. "You are way too dressed."

Cassidy smirked, "Let me fix that for ya." She pulled her t-shirt over her head, then her sports bra, shoes, and jeans came off. Imari licked her lips as she stared at all of that lean muscle on display. Her eyes stopped at Cassidy's small breasts and at those perky nipples that were already hard.

Imari sat up on her knees, her hands sliding down Cassidy's taut stomach. Her lover shivered under the touch, and Imari kissed her. Cassidy groaned as Imari delved into her mouth at the same time Imari's fingers slid between her legs. Her thumb pulled apart Cassidy's pussy lips to swipe at her lover's hard clit.

Cassidy bucked, "Yes."

Imari slipped her fingers inside, and it was hot and tight around her thick fingers. She plundered Cassidy's depths as she increased the pressure of her thumb against Cassidy's clit.

Imari let go of Cassidy's mouth, Cassidy's hips bucking so violently against her that Imari thought she was going to knock her down.

"Harder," Cassidy said, tipping her head back, long black hair spilling over her back. "Fuck me... fuck me harder."

Imari increased the pace. Her lips darted down, sucked on the column of her throat, and then down to latch on a nipple. Imari decided it was high time to give Cassidy a dose of her own medicine and gave the nub a hard suck.

Cassidy arched, mouth falling open into a silent scream as she came. Imari thought it was the most sublime thing she had ever seen.

Imari pulled her down onto the bed. Cassidy lay down, her dark hair fanning out around her like a curtain.

"Fuck," she said, panting for breath.

Imari's boldness left her suddenly, and she bit her lip as she stared down at Cassidy.

"Was it—" Imari coughed. "Was it good?"

Cassidy's mouth split into a wide smile. "It was more than good; it was magnificent."

With a put-upon sigh, Imari adjusted herself to lie next to Cassidy. She laid her head on top of the other woman's chest, and Cassidy pulled the covers over them.

Imari sighed again as Cassidy wrapped her arms around her. Cassidy leaned up and took her lips in a slow and sweet kiss. They just lay there for a moment, kissing and enjoying the feel of their naked bodies pressed together.

Time seemed to stretch on, wrapped in the bubble of Imari's bedroom, only broken up with kisses, soft laughter, and a feeling of utter contentment.

And then it grew into something hotter. The caress of fingers across sweat-slicked skin, the nip of a mouth, the rock of hips, and the slide into arousal that built gradually into a flame that was less urgent than earlier.

With a shift of a leg, Cassidy was slotting her leg between Imari's own. She pressed up against Imari's clit. Imari groaned as they rocked together, fingers lacing each other as they rocked.

It was unrushed, just a slow slide that itched her desire higher. Pleasure raced down her spine, and Imari twisted, meeting Cassidy's hips.

"Yeah, just like that baby," Cassidy murmured into her lips before she kissed her again. "Come with me."

One rock of the hips, then two, and Imari threw her head back. Cassidy bucked up against her as they both came apart simultaneously in each other arms.

Imari slumped back down, and Cassidy kissed her forehead.

"I think you wore me out," Imari said tiredly.

Cassidy just chuckled and held her tighter. Imari knew she should go and at least get a towel to clean up a bit, but she felt so safe and comfortable in Cassidy's arms. She nuzzled between her lover's breasts and then gradually fell into a peaceful sleep.

Chapter Seven

Where are the songs of spring? Ay, Where are they?
Think not of them, thou hast thy music too,—
While barred clouds bloom the soft-dying day,
And touch the stubble-plains with rosy hue;
— To Autumn by John Keats

Imari woke to the sensation of fur against her nose. She wrinkled her nose and batted Bramble's tail away from her. Bramble sat on her chest, glaring down at her.

Imari sighed. "You are hungry, right?"

Bramble just sat there, staring at her creepily, and Imari groaned. Imari tentatively put her hand out to pet him. She sighed in relief as her cat didn't immediately try to bite her fingers off.

Imari gave him a few ears scritches and then looked over to the side. Cassidy was gone, and Imari's shoulder slumped in disappointment.

Imari gave her cat a few more ears scritches as she looked over at the empty space beside her. The door was left open by a crack. Cassidy must have left while Imari had still been sleeping.

She had been looking forward to waking up with her lover.

Imari shooed Bramble away and sat up in bed. It was best to feed Bramble before the cat knocked over something expensive in revenge.

Imari jumped when Cassidy was suddenly walking through the door, holding a tray of delicious breakfast foods and two steaming coffee cups.

"Good morning." Cassidy smiled softly as she set down the tray on Imari's lap and bent down to give her a sweet kiss.

"Morning."

Bramble gave a pointed meow, and they both broke apart. "I think my cock blocking us is going to be a thing."

"This is what the lord made locked doors for," Imari giggled. "Besides, he's just hungry."

"I was going to feed him, but I didn't know how to fix it correctly, and I know from experience cats are very particular about that."

Imari quickly gave Cassidy directions. She tried to tell Cassidy that she didn't have to do it, but the other woman just kissed her again and left with Bramble hot on her heels.

Imari looked over all the food. It included eggs, bacon, and pancakes that had fruit slices with a smiley face on top of them. Imari couldn't help the wide, cheerful grin. It seemed like the magic of last night wasn't temporary, after all.

And she hoped that meant that this would never end.

As if on cue, a familiar ringtone played. It surprised Imari that her phone still had any battery life left at all. With shaking hands, she picked up the phone, and sure enough, it was her mom.

Imari's hands hovered between the decline and accept buttons. She bit her lip, took a deep breath, and then she pushed decline.

Then Imari finally blocked her mother.

Zephyr had been right. She deserved to be happy, and Cassidy made her feel truly adored. She would not let her mother ruin her happiness anymore.

Cassidy came back in and sat down next to her. Imari leaned forward and gave Cassidy a long, lingering kiss.

"What was that for?"

"Just for you being you," Imari said.

Cassidy took her hand and brushed her lips against her knuckles. "I hope you know I don't want this to be a one-night thing. "Cassidy took a deep breath. "I think it's too soon for the L-word, but I do have feelings for you, and I want to see where that goes."

"I feel the same," Imari said as she squeezed her hand. "Besides, I would be foolish to let you slip through my fingers, again."

Cassidy laughed, and in the morning's sunlight with her happiness in her own hands, Imari knew she'd made the right choice.

Epilogue

And full-grown lambs loud bleat from hilly bourn;
Hedge-crickets sing; and now with treble soft
The red-breast whistles from a garden-croft;
And gathering swallows twitter in the skies.
— To Autumn by John Keats

"Okay folks," Cassidy said as she sat at the head of the table. "Before we eat, we have to say what we're grateful for."

Peyton groaned. "Come on. Just because your parents went on vacation doesn't mean you have to continue this tradition."

"A tradition is a tradition." Cassidy shrugged.

Imari laughed, "It's not that bad, and besides, Thanksgiving is all about gratitude."

"I agree." Cassidy nodded. "Besides, it's only going to take five minutes."

"But I have been waiting to eat all day," Peyton whined. She looked pointedly at the turkey, then at the collard greens, stuffing, and macaroni and cheese. "And these all look so good."

Imari turned to Zephyr, whose entire attention was on his phone. "Zephyr?"

"What?" Zephyr looked up to see the gaze of the entire table was on him.

"What are you grateful for?"

Zephyr slid his phone into his pocket and grinned. "I am grateful for the hot date I have with Elliot on Saturday!"

The table groaned.

Zephyr shrugged. "It's true."

Cassidy looked pointedly at Peyton, and they rolled their eyes. "I'm grateful for the semester for being almost over..."

"Well, I'm thankful for thoughtful employees." Cassidy turned and smiled at Imari. "And bumping into the best thing that's ever happened to me."

Imari grinned back at the woman who had shaken her life upside down in the best way. "And I am grateful for all of you showing me what real family is."

Her gaze traveled around to the table, stopping at Cassidy and right into those loving eyes, and Imari knew that this was only the beginning of a life filled with true acceptance and love.

THE END

Acknowledgments

I want to thank my mother, who, even from the very beginning, fostered and encouraged my love of reading buying books, and then later pushing me to become a professional author. She believed in me when I thought it was a pipe dream I could write anything at all because of my ADHD and serve dyslexia. I also want to thank my best friends Tris and her wife Robyn for cheering me on from the sidelines, and my partner Starr, who cheered for this book louder than anyone else.

I also want to thank all my friends on social media, especially my fellow Black LGBTQ+ authors who supported, uplifted me, and in my darkest moments told me I could finish this book (which is the longest one I have written to date). I want to especially thank Ivy Quinn for editing this book and Rivulet027 for the fantastic betaing job. Finally, I want to thank

Tamara Lush for coming in my time of need and for formatting this book.

The Devil's Bargain
by Rian Fox

When a rare first edition book from a famous 19th century Occultist ends up in Silas lap at an auction, life as he knows it suddenly changes. Pressured into performing one of the rituals from the book by a friend, Silas gets a tease of regret. Now Silas can't sleep, is having nightmares that end with him waking up terrified. Something obscene, dark and deadly wants Silas and he isn't human.

Bazaduil lusts for Silas and won't take no for an answer, even if it means tricking and seducing him. In a life where being told 'there are no monsters,' it will be one lie Silas will have to face. Will Silas be able to ignore Bazaduil advances or will he submit to this demon's twisted agenda

About Author

Georgina Kiersten (Rian Fox) is a black non-binary author who was raised in San Antonio, Texas. Living with a disability has given Georgina the ability to see the world in a unique and open way that shines through their writing. When they not writing and reading the latest books, Georgina is a graphic designer by trade and a bit of a geek diving headfirst into the fandom universe. As well as juggling five kids and two dogs. Look for more of Georgina's books in the future, specialized in racially diverse LGBTQ romance and erotica.

Support The Author

If you enjoyed this book, please consider leaving a review. A review really helps other people to find my book and it's a great way to support a Black independent author. If you want more snippets from my upcoming works, behind the scenes looks into my writing process, and get exclusive sales on my upcoming book please subscribe to my free newsletter at georginakiersten.com/subscribe.